The First D[illegible] Homeschool

Written by Michelle Fredrickson
Illustrated by Jenny Carlisle

ISBN 978-1490977942

First Edition

www.thenatureofgrace.blogspot.com

For my amazing children -
you + homeschool = the inspiration for this book!
I love you SOOO much!
- M. F.

For my own little elves, Joshua and Lillian.
-J.C.

Where is
Homeschool Elf?

He is hiding behind the red shirt.

What is the opposite of "dawn"?

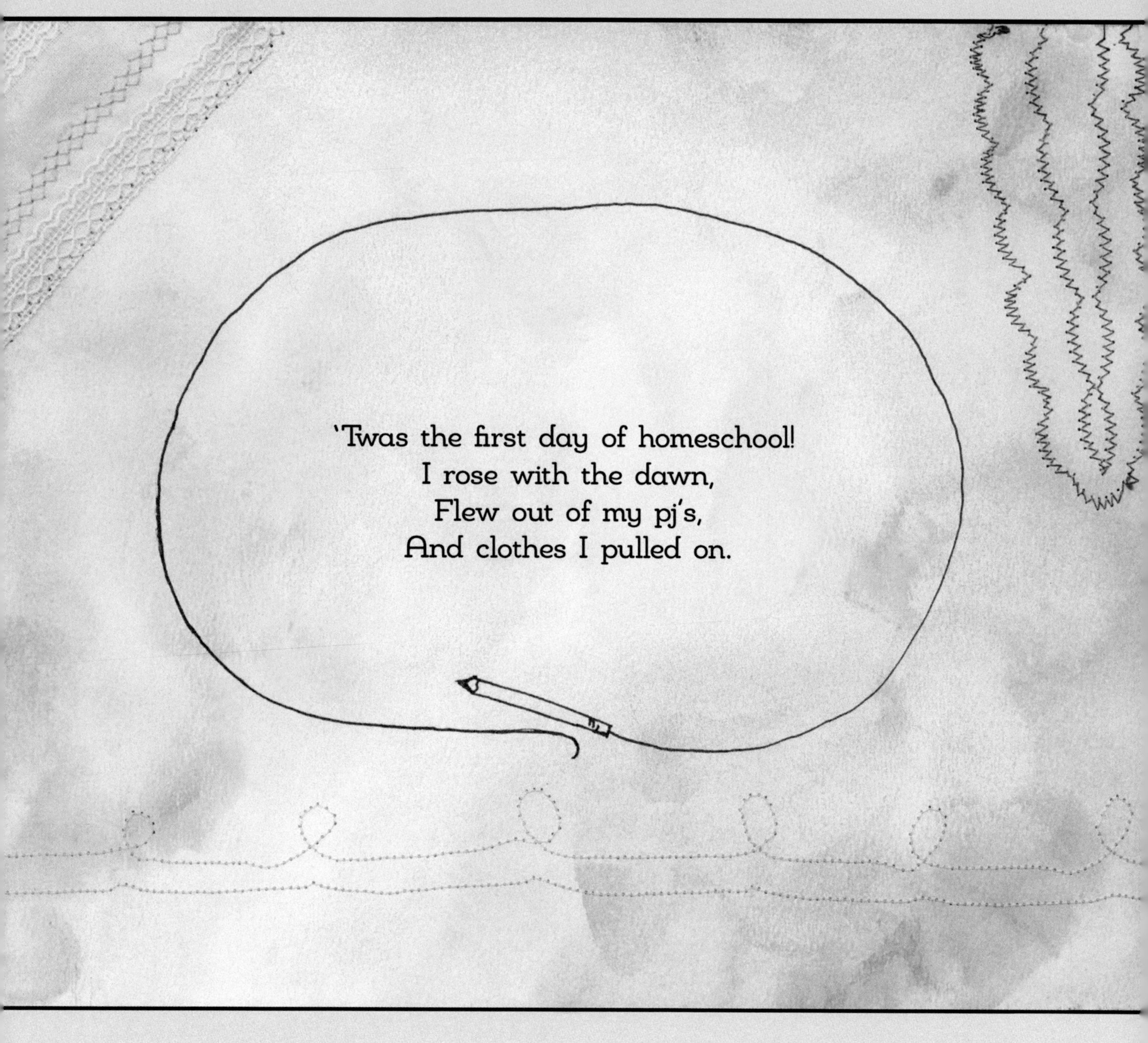

Where is
Homeschool Elf?

He is hiding behind the table and pot.

How do you feel on the first day of homeschool? Why?

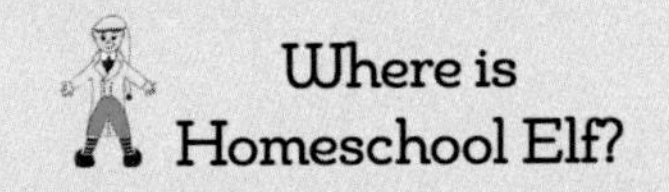

He is hiding under the table.

What do you think the word "flit" means?

My feet, how they flit
To the dining room table.
My wiggles contained,
(Though just barely able).

My sister and brother
Did finally appear,
And breakfast we ate
With much laughter and cheer!

Where is Homeschool Elf?

He is hiding behind the counter (sink).

What is something you can do to help after a meal?

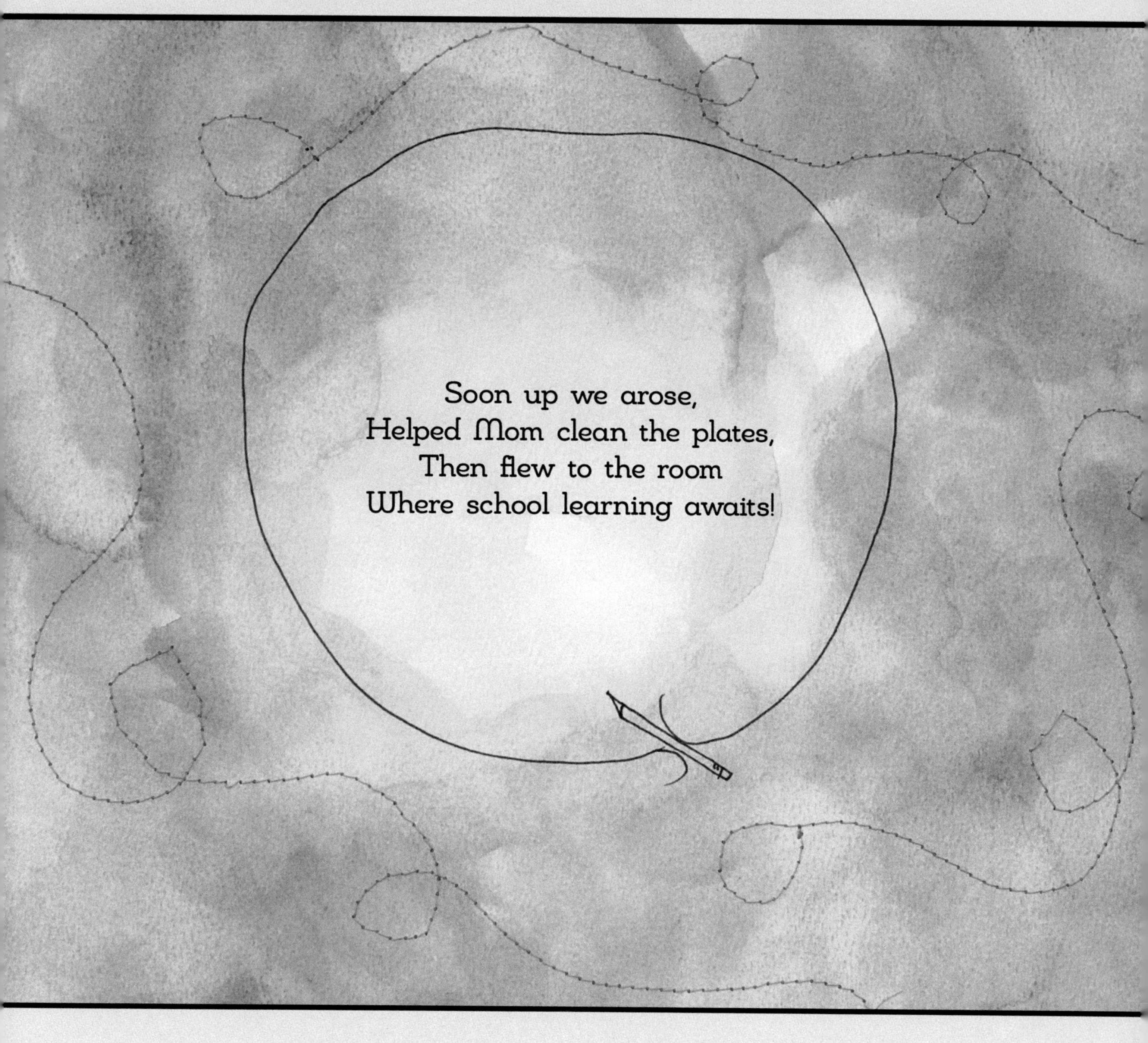

Where is Homeschool Elf?

He is hiding behind the globe on page 9 and behind the books on page 10.

There were maps on the wall
And a globe on the shelf.
But our books and supplies?
Snitched by Homeschool Elf!

What fun things do you do on your first day of homeschool?

He left us some clues,
And we solved one by one
Til we found what we sought.
My, that hunt was such fun!

Oh, the smell of new pencils,
Erasers, and more!
The shiny new covers of
Schoolbooks galore!

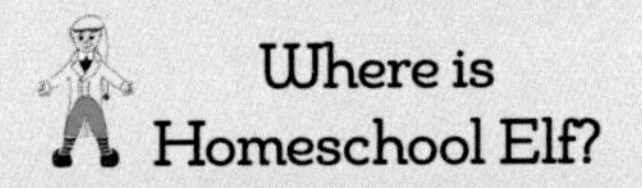

Where is Homeschool Elf?

He is hiding behind the table.

Why do you think it is important to learn?

We settled right down
To read and to write,
To study and study
With all of our might!

Mom worked with us all,
One on one helped us learn.
Chores and studies we finished,
While each waited a turn.

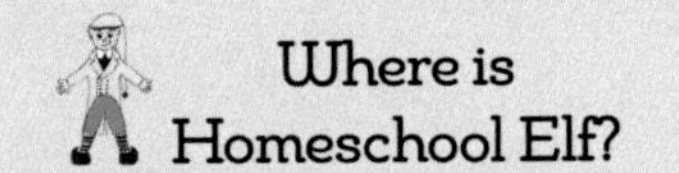

Where is
Homeschool Elf?

He is hiding under the table on page 13
and behind the daddy's leg on page 14.

Lunch came and it went,

And while Mom planned more days,

We had quiet time

And then helped in big ways!

What are some ways you can help your mom and dad?

Where is Homeschool Elf?

He is hiding behind the barn.

Why is it important to learn how to be a good friend?

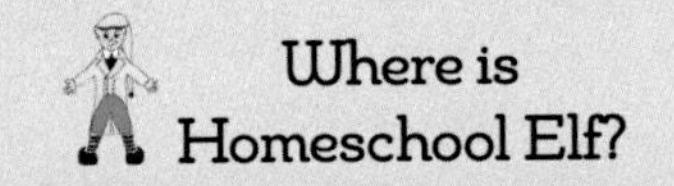

He is hiding in the corner by the cat.

What kinds of things do you do to get ready for bed at night?

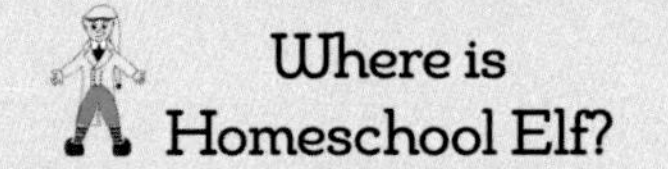

He is hiding behind the arm of the sofa on page 19 and under the bed on page 20.

Hugs and kisses from loved ones
Completed the night.
We read books together

Then out went the light.

I thought of tomorrow
And the year up ahead.
Dreamed of what I'd achieve,
As I lay in my bed.

What is your favorite part of homeschool?

Homeschool Elf Pattern:

Start your own tradition with Homeschool Elf!
Copy this page, color your elf (or use the one already colored), cut him out, and decide how you want to involve him in your homeschool!

Made in the USA
Lexington, KY
09 September 2019